That afternoon in our garden perhaps we played being Jews, fighting with wicked German soldiers, after we were tired of being valiant French soldiers and dying. Pierre and I found twigs ourselves, and began to parry and feint like professional swordsmen. René's gun shot at us several times, but as we refused to fall down dead, the gun became a dagger, and we tussled with heroic strength.

"Well, well," said a voice, "such imaginative children."

We paused in our play, breathing hard.

Two German soldiers stood in the passageway at the side of the house, looking over the gate at us.

OTHER BOOKS BY GREGORY MAGUIRE

———— ❧ ————

THE HAMLET CHRONICLES:

SEVEN SPIDERS SPINNING

SIX HAUNTED HAIRDOS

FIVE ALIEN ELVES

FOUR STUPID CUPIDS

The Good Liar

GREGORY MAGUIRE

HARPERTROPHY®
An Imprint of HarperCollins*Publishers*

Harper Trophy® is a registered trademark of
HarperCollins Publishers Inc.

The Good Liar

Library of Congress Cataloging-in-Publication Data
Maguire, Gregory.
The good liar / Gregory Maguire.— 1st HarperTrophy ed.
p. cm.
Reprint. Originally published: Dublin, Ireland : The O'Brien Press, 1995; first published
in the U.S.: New York : Clarion Books, 1999.
Summary: Now an old man living in the United States, Marcel recalls his childhood in
German-occupied France, especially the summer that he and his older brother René
befriended a young German soldier.
ISBN 0-06-440874-4 (pbk.)
1. World War, 1939–1945—France—Juvenile fiction. [1. World War, 1939–1945—France—
Fiction. 2. France—History—German occupation, 1940–1945—Fiction.] I. Title.
PZ7.M2762Go 2002   2001051454
[Fic]—dc21   CIP
                                                                    AC

First Harper Trophy edition, 2002
Visit us on the World Wide Web!
www.harperchildrens.com

For Margaret O'Brien
and for Mary and Maureen—
Liberté! Egalité! Sororité!—
and also, of course,
for Brendan

The author thanks Suzette and Jean-Marc Tanis-Plant
and their sons, Michael and Paul, for hospitality, roast
rabbit with an exquisite mustard sauce, bonhomie,
and crucial help with critical details of this book.
Thanks as well to Rafique Keshavjee for a keen eye,
patience, and a capable grasp of French; the research
in the Loire Valley was made that much more
pleasant. Finally, thanks to the citizens of small
villages near Cerelles, north of Tours.

The Good Liar is a work of fiction and does not
portray any actual people, living or dead.

CONTENTS

The Good Liar

Dear Mr. Delarue,

Our class is studying World War II in Europe. We have to do a project. We're supposed to talk to an old person about it. This is Florida, so everybody goes: Lots of old folks here! No sweat! But everybody old we ask, they say during the war they were living in New York, New York. They all want to tell us about victory gardens and collecting tin cans. All the old ladies with blue hair and scarves and sunglasses, they all collected tin when they were our age. That's all they say.

But yesterday when we were trying to find the Disney Channel on TV, we found this other show instead. You were on it. You were showing your paintings, all trees and bridges. You said you grew up in France during the war. That's what you painted. Trees and bridges from when you were small. You sure *look* old enough. No offense.

So could you please tell us these things, please, so we can get an A?

1

1. Are you old enough to remember your childhood and the war? But not so old that you forget everything?

2. Did you see anything good and gross like in the movies?

3. Did you do anything awesome like hide gold under your sled to foil the Nazis?

(This isn't a question.) We really like studying the war. It's the best thing so far this year. Please tell us what it was like.

If the TV channel forwards this letter!

Your fans,
Maria Diaz
Meg Mueller
Reenie-Tawnetta Price
(in alphabetical order).

P.S. Your paintings were very talented.
P.P.S. We're at the Robert F. Kennedy School, Mr. Wimmel's class.
P.P.P.S. It has to get here by April 1st.
P.P.P.P.S. Many thanx!

Dear Maria, Meg, and Reenie-Tawnetta,

You are in luck. The people at the television studio sent your letter on to me right away. I have lived in America since the early 1950s, but you are right: I grew up in Europe. I didn't know we were so rare!

So I hurry to answer your questions.

Now is this good luck for you or is it bad luck? Last month my daughter Monique gave me her old word processor. For four weeks I have sat on the porch with the thing on my knobby knees, teaching myself how to make it behave. (You know all about such things. Now, so do I.) So I can answer your questions.

But the bad luck is this. I can't answer your questions one-two-three. They would not tell you anything. Watch.

1. Yes

2. No.

3. Define *awesome.* Awesome to whom?

I am embarrassed to admit the selfishness of memory. While I knew the war was going on—we lived in France, a village called Mont-Saint-Martin, in the Loire Valley—my childhood was mostly like heaven, the way childhood should be. I cannot help it. Your teacher might be disappointed in me, and so might you.

Your letter arrived last week. I slept, and I dreamed rich dreams of long ago. I was remembering those days, thanks to your questions. I will write about them for you. But you will find that I killed no Nazi soldiers when I was a boy. Nor have I killed anyone, ever since.

I'm used to naming things. I name paintings all the time. *Cow with Bridge. Cow with Trees. Cow with Bridge, Trees, Two Ducks, and a Broken Bicycle.* So I will name this letter. I will call it *The Good Liar*. Not because I am telling lies here!

But because memory of long ago is fuzzy. It goes in and out of focus. It is like a picture fading in strong sunlight. One day blends into another, so all you remember are what days were like on the average. Except when something rare happens. Then it's like fresh wet paint on white canvas! Oil paints smell strong—you can never forget the power of alizarin crimson, burnt umber, cadmium orange. Paint marks your hands unless you scrub them with turpentine. Memory rushes together into a general vague summary, unless and until something rare and novel happens. Then memory tries to hold it bright and new, like a new bright mark of paint on canvas.

I will tell you about Maman, about Uncle Anton, about Pierre and René and me, Fat Marcel. I will try to make my memory work as if I am painting from it. Maybe it will help if I break my memories into sections, and give them names, as I name my paintings. The first one would be called "The Letter." And I can date it pretty clearly. It must have been 1940. For Paris was falling to the Germans.

1

The Letter

It starts with Maman.

She was reading a letter, standing in the doorway of our house.

"Boys!" called Maman. "Boys, come here at once!"

We had finished schooling for the year, so we were playing in the garden. We came shouting and shoving up to the step on which she stood, page in hand. Even our dog Mirabeau came and waited with her tongue hanging.

"A letter," she said, "a letter you have to listen to." Her voice was firm and wavery at once, in a way we had never heard before. It made us nervous.

"Is it from Papa?" asked Pierre, who was the oldest, about twelve. He wore glasses and looked through them at things, like a lost baby owl. "Is he coming home soon?"

"It is not from Papa," said Maman, and she straightened her spine and threw her shoulders back. Papa was working somewhere far away, sending his pay home to us. We all missed him. Maman made a good effort not to show that she missed him, but we children knew that she did.

"Well who is it from?" asked René behind me, poking me in the ribs and pretending he hadn't. He looked all innocent when I turned around and scowled. René was the middle boy, about ten. He was a rascal: clever, impatient, full of fun and disobedience. He was blond and bony, always wearing through his shirtsleeves and the knees of his trousers. I idolized him.

"It is from your uncle Anton." (The telephones had not yet gotten to us. Letter writing was the way we kept in touch.) "Uncle Anton lives in Montmartre, in Paris. Do you remember? Listen, boys, attend to me now. This is important. He writes that the German soldiers are heading toward Paris. He writes that the German army swarmed through Belgium and Holland a month ago, and they are now swarming through France. No one knows what will happen next."

Pierre looked sober and worried, and said, "This is bad." But René was impatient. "We already *know* this, Maman. We remember the day a few weeks ago. The church bell rang, and our studies were interrupted. War was declared! You went to church to pray, and we stayed at home and were good boys."

"You were not good boys," scolded Maman, about to get distracted. "You were supposed to stay inside, and you went running through the lanes playing soldiers. The neighbors all complained about your noise. I was embarrassed, and I was angry that you lied to me when I came home. But that is not the point now. You have already been punished for that."

"I remember," said René, pretending his bum was still sore. Maman believed in spanking.

"Why don't we hear from Papa more often?" said Pierre, biting his upper lip.

"Pierre, *attend*," said Maman. She knew that even

though Pierre was her oldest son, he was not very smart, and he needed to be talked to very clearly. She continued: "René, stop acting like a monkey and listen. Marcel, even you need to hear this. Are you boys listening?"

"Yes, Maman," we said, trying to behave.

"Of course we're listening," said René dismissively, "but Marcel is too young to understand, and Pierre is too foolish, so you might as well just say it to me."

Maman hit him on the arm.

It was not unusual for René to be sassy. It *was* unusual for Maman to strike anyone, except for the occasional spanking on our rear ends. We stopped clowning around and listened. René rubbed his arm and sulked.

"Uncle Anton may be coming with some friends," she told us. "Some friends from Paris. A woman and her little girl. They may stay with us for a few days. I do not want you to tell anyone they are here. The Germans could be heading south after taking Paris. They might come through town and ask lots of questions. We will not say that Uncle Anton and his friends have come for a visit. We will especially not say anything in front of Madame Sevremont in the village store!"

"Why not?" we asked. Madame Sevremont was a toothless old gossip. Well-meaning, but dim as a hen. She sat in her chair at the doorway of her store looking out across the Place du 11 Novembre, and she saw everyone coming and going. She broadcast what she saw without shame or restraint. We liked her, and we didn't think very seriously about her.

"What our family does is no business of Madame Sevremont's," said Maman.

"But she always knows when everyone comes and goes in town," we said. Madame Sevremont served as a sort of volunteer message service.

"She cannot keep a secret," replied Maman. "Even when she snores, she blurts small private matters aloud."

"Really?" we said. "How do you know?"

"I am exaggerating to make a point," she said. "I mean that she has no self-control."

"You told a lie!" said René gleefully.

"René, will you *attend*!" said Maman, at the end

11

of her patience. But she had lost us. We fell to giggling over Maman's exaggeration. With a little, bitten-off word of annoyance, Maman took the letter inside, to try again later, when we'd got over our silliness. When three boys are growing up in the same family, there is a lot of silliness, and sometimes it gets in the way of important matters.

2
Liars!

Why did we giggle as poor Maman struggled to get us to take Uncle Anton's letter seriously?

You see, we boys had a passion for lying. Like many French families, we were Roman Catholics, but Maman was an especially religious person. Daily she read the Bible and her prayer books, and she trained us to behave in the old-fashioned way. Courtesy to our elders. Quiet on Sunday. Church services were the main entertainment; we had no cinema in our village, and we were too young to read for long hours.

Before he left for such a long time, our father had forbidden us to lie anymore. "My boys," he had said to us, "it will be hard on you and on your dear maman for me to be so far away. You must always tell the truth and behave. I do not like this tangle of fibs and stories you weave. To be French is to be honest and direct."

"Yes, Papa," we said, and we kissed him good-bye and cried. And then after he left, each one of us boys lied to the others and said that we had *not* cried. Maman softened her airy expression of goodness. She knew we would miss our father terribly. He had never been away before. But she reminded us, when we got too imaginative, "Boys, never lie. The priest says so, I say so, and so does your father. His heart would break if he knew."

But we were children. And while we knew we would never kill, or steal, we needed *one* law to break. It was impossible to be *perfect*. So we were liars. Pierre, René, and Fat Marcel: the biggest and best liars in Mont-Saint-Martin. We had been practicing for ages.

We did not mean to be bad. Nor were there rules to our brotherly game. No method of scoring, no selecting a winner. We simply tried to lie—

inventively, persuasively—whenever we could. We just amused ourselves.

"Madame Sevremont is a thousand years old. She sleeps in a coffin," said René once, as we balanced on the stone wall of our garden.

"No," said Pierre, "she is only five hundred years old. She is a baby, and her mother sleeps in a coffin. She sleeps in a well." He fell off the wall.

"She isn't really old," I tried. "She is actually a teenage girl. She just drinks old medicine every day. She only looks like an old lady, for she is in disguise."

"She's a spy for the Germans," said René.

"She's a spy for the gargoyles and the devils in hell," said Pierre.

"She's a spy for the grown-ups," I said.

"Who are you talking about?" asked Maman, coming to toss some water on the vegetables.

"A woman I saw on the street yesterday," said René.

"I hope you're not making up tales about our neighbors," said Maman. "I do not like it when you lie. Your father would not like it either."

I guess you can see: Sometimes our lying was just inventing stories. Other times our lying was to hide the truth. And it is those times that our lying got us into trouble. Like the time of spilt milk and stolen irises.

3
Spilt Milk
and Stolen Irises

Coming back one evening from the farm where we went to get milk, Pierre, René, and I began to run. Mirabeau pranced alongside us, yapping her delight. Pierre swung the milk pail around in a circle, and the milk stayed inside. This seemed a miracle to me!

"How does it do that?" I asked. I was too young to understand the force of centrifugal motion. "Let me try."

"You're too small," said René.

"Oh, let him try," said Pierre, peering at me kindly through his spectacles. (He had inherited them from the village doctor when the doctor died. It had been hoped that seeing better might make him a little smarter, but that hope was soon dashed.)

"He'll get us into trouble," said René.

I *was* too small to get up enough speed to swing the milk pail. When Pierre let me try, the milk went slopping out over the road, splashing the dark wild weeds with dripping mustaches. I remember the milk even dotting the fretwork of a spider's web with tiny pearly drops, small as bugs' teeth.

This was a serious loss. There wasn't enough milk to waste in accidents, nor money for replacing it. Especially since our father was away. Legally, it was all my fault; *I* had spilled the milk. Luckily, as the youngest I should get the lightest punishment. But Pierre and René felt bad. After all, *they* had swung the pail first. *They* had urged me to take a try. We chattered in fear, the threat of our angry mother more real and terrible to us than the threat of the approaching German army. Would it be possible to avoid punishment altogether?

"Think, René," commanded Pierre, who had

draped his arm on my shoulder to cheer me up. He was strong and good to me.

René thought. Then we made a detour. When we arrived back in our kitchen, we had a milk pail filled with opening iris blossoms. "Look," we chorused with our fake enthusiasm, "look what the nuns gave us!"

"Where's our milk?" asked Maman suspiciously.

"Oh, Mother Superior saw us on the road and begged us to give her the milk!" René was glib as a mockingbird. "They had a very, very, *very* sick nun who needed fresh milk right away. The mother superior gave us flowers from her garden to thank us for our Christian charity!"

We knew Maman approved of Christian charity. We thought we might be safe if an excess of Christian charity were the only thing we were guilty of.

"The nuns have a cow of their own," said Maman, but she recognized the irises as being the deep purple kind that grew only in the convent garden. They were admired by all the villagers.

"Their cow is sick too," said René. "Maybe whatever the sick nun has is contagious." He had a very worried expression on his face. Pierre and I knew he was not sure this lie would work.

But Maman said in her kindly way, "If the poor nun is so sick, perhaps I should go over with my medicine basket." She had a way with sick people and animals. She kept ready a basket woven from rushes in which she stored gauze, tape, pills, and herbs. Also a Bible for comfort.

"Oh no," said René hurriedly, pretending a huge interest in arranging the irises in a jar. "Mother Superior said the poor old nun was *very very* contagious, and no one was to come near. It's a quarantine. That was why they couldn't go out and get more milk from the farm themselves. They called to us over the wall, and slid the flowers through the iron gate."

Maman coolly observed the three of us. We stared back, looking as honest and innocent as we could. We were good at that! Lots of practice.

We almost got away with it. René's lie had just enough lifelike detail to convince Maman. But the next day when our mother went to the shop, old Madame Sevremont said, "Did you hear about the horrid vandalism in the convent garden?

Someone climbed over the wall and broke off those rare irises, every single one!"

We were punished mightily for this. René tried even at this late moment to appeal to our mother's sense of justice. "We were only trying to protect Fat Marcel! It was all his fault that the milk got spilt." But to Maman brotherly love was no excuse for lying. I do not know if it is possible that all three of us were laid over her knees at once and hit on our bare bottoms. This is how I remember it, anyway.

4

Soldiers

Our house was an ordinary stone building, nei-
ther an elegant spun-sugar chateau nor a damp
hovel. The unpainted stucco was the color of
beech bark, warm and severe at once, and the corners of the building were outlined in a pattern of
rosy bricks. The window shutters, once green, had
faded to gray. Most homes in Mont-Saint-Martin
fronted the street, with the gardens, if they had
them, in back. Ours looked like most, but our garden was on the side, behind a low wall in the slow
act of falling down. If you looked at the house
from across the road, the front elevation was
roughly the shape of an L: a tall red-roofed stack of
rooms on the left, and a low wing running off to

the right. The parlor and kitchen occupied the ground floor, and the two bedrooms were one level up. Below the kitchen was a small, dank cellar for storing fruits and vegetables Maman put up in glass jars for the winter. A little, dusty attic hung between the rafters above Maman's bedroom. The wing on the right held the entrance hall.

I was helping Maman take something from the attic one day when the door burst open down below and Pierre came running through the house. "Paris is gone!" he shouted. "I heard at the café, Paris has fallen today!"

Maman sat down at the top of the ladder. "Oh, Marcel," she said to me as if I were grown-up. "Now there'll be trouble."

She didn't even yell at Pierre, who was forbidden to go to the café. Stupid Pierre hadn't even bothered to lie about where he'd heard this awful news. But it didn't seem to matter. Paris had fallen. And only a few days later France surrendered to Nazi Germany. We had lost the war.

But nothing changed for a while, until the day I spent at Maman's heels, playing with tiny extra scraps of dough. I drew pictures in the flour that she sprinkled on the old warped worktable. Maman had set some sort of a fruit pie on the broad stone edge of the outdoor sink in the kitchen yard. It was cooling and smelling most appetizing. Pierre and René came home from their piano lesson, and we were playing in the garden. Mirabeau was asleep on the sunny doorstep.

Maman called, "Look after yourselves while I go out to see the sick baby over at the seamstress's. And do not go running in the lanes. And do not lie to me about it when I ask you what you have done." She then strode off with her medicine basket, wearing the wooden clogs some country people still wore, because the day had been rainy and the roads were rutted with mud.

A fruit pie was a very rare treat then. Perhaps it was a *jour de fête*—a saint's day, a name day—or maybe visitors were planned. Or perhaps it was for Uncle Anton, who was expected any day but seemed never to arrive. I can't remember. But we began to play a game of soldiers. We played Soldiers and Martyrs. René was a German soldier with a perfectly shaped stick for a rifle. Pierre and

I were valiant French soldiers willing to die for France.

You see, we lived in the depths of Touraine—the center of France—isolated in the quiet heartland of the country. Nevertheless, all we talked about was what was happening in Germany and France. We couldn't get enough of war news. We didn't know how bad it would get, of course. We didn't know about concentration camps, for instance—they hadn't been begun yet in France. But we knew Jews had been attacked in Germany. Uncle Anton had written to us what he read in the Paris newspapers. Jewish stores had been smashed. We were glad it was so far away—but it wasn't as far away as we'd have liked.

At that time most French Jews lived in the big cities. But though it was hardly a common thing in rural France, our little village of Mont-Saint-Martin had its own small population of Jews— maybe ten or fourteen. They lived together in a villa clawed over with dark vines. Old Madame Sevremont told everyone that a rabbi from Poland had moved in there, and the rest were his family or his followers. There were occasional comings and goings of friends. They seemed strange and intense to us, because of their dark dress and foreign ways, and because they spoke little or no French. Why the rabbi had come to Mont-Saint-Martin I never learned. Perhaps he had had some inkling of how bad things would become in the cities.

Madame Sevremont knew everything and told everything. To everyone. "The Jews from Poland are here because they had to flee from Poland," she said to us once. "Times are hard for Jews there, and in Germany. Are you kids going to buy something, or are you just looking?"

"Why are times hard for Jews?" asked Pierre.

"It's beyond your understanding," said Madame Sevremont kindly—she knew Pierre was slow. "It's beyond mine, too," she admitted, almost to herself.

That afternoon in our garden perhaps we played being Jews, fighting with wicked German soldiers, after we were tired of being valiant French soldiers and dying. Pierre and I found twigs ourselves, and began to parry and feint like professional swordsmen. René's gun shot at us several times, but as we refused to fall down dead, the gun became a dagger, and we tussled with heroic strength.

"Well, well," said a voice, "such imaginative children."

We paused in our play, breathing hard.

Two German soldiers stood in the passageway at the side of the house, looking over the gate at us. Mirabeau opened one eye and growled faintly.

Two real German soldiers, with gray eyes and golden hair.

The French spoken by the friendly soldier was funny, but we could understand it. The other soldier didn't look at us. He seemed unwell.

"I am searching for the woman who is a doctor," said the French-speaking soldier. "I am told she lives here."

So the Germans had come to Mont-Saint-Martin. Already!

Pierre adjusted his glasses and said anxiously, "Well, you see—"

"Whoever told you that?" interrupted René, bounding up to the gate. I think he was terrified. But he was so relieved that the soldier had a friendly voice that he was electrified into action. This was our first German. He was very polite; somehow he reminded me of our father.

"The woman at the pharmacy said we should come here. My companion is sick, and we need some advice." The other soldier looked as if he might topple over.

"She is not here," said Pierre, who, while a capable liar when he thought of it, had a tendency to tell the truth to adults, especially to adults who frightened him.

"Pierre!" said René. He elbowed our older brother away from the gate and took up the front position. "Our maman is in Chinon taking care of our sick grandmother," said René with conviction.

Pierre and I were dumbfounded. Our grandmother in Chinon had not been in need of our maman's attentions for several years, since she was entirely dead.

I said, "Very sick, very sick, very very sick grandmother. She throws up every fifteen minutes."

"Her eyes roll about in her head like a crazy per-

son," said René confidentially. "I hope it's not contagious."

"When she throws up, it's not pretty," I said.
"It looks like—"

"I see," said the German quickly.

Pierre took off his spectacles and polished them
on his shirt, speechless.

"We are very sorry," said René. "We hope your
friend is better soon. But now we must study our
lessons. Come on, brothers."

We raced into the kitchen and appeared imme-
diately at the window, staring ferociously at our
soldier. He snapped a military salute and allowed
his friend to slump against his shoulder. He half
walked, half dragged his friend away.

"He's very sick," said Pierre.

"I think he's very drunk," said René, and he
was probably right.

The two soldiers disappeared around the bend
in the lane.

"We'd better go out and fasten the gate," said
René. "Quick. No one's around."

"No," said Pierre. "I'm the oldest and I say
NO."

"I'm the youngest and I say NO too," I said.

"I'm the middle and I don't care what you say," said René casually. So with René in the lead, we allowed ourselves to race back into the yard and fasten the gate. Then, in a flurry of excitement, we played our fencing game all the more furiously. Around and around the yard we raced, crushing flowers, lunging, dropping to the ground, yelling like wild animals. When we got tired, we paused to rest, dropping right on the path and sitting there like three exhausted puppies. Mirabeau licked us one after the other.

"I think we'd better not tell Maman that the soldiers came," said Pierre.

"Why not?" said René.

"She would worry about us if she knew soldiers were around. She has enough worrying."

"*You* worry too much," said René. "You're so stiff all the time." He tickled Pierre until Pierre's glasses fell off, and Pierre howled for mercy. I helped with the tickling. I was always on the side of whichever older brother was winning at the moment.

5
Maman Is Angry

Maman came home an hour later. Miraculously, her trip to the seamstress and back had not taken her within sight of the column of German soldiers. She didn't know what amazements had happened while she was away.

We would not tell her that German soldiers had been looking for her! We would protect her. And this would make our father proud of us and love us.

But before we could enjoy our own kind natures, Maman launched a conversation.

"Who knocked our pie into the sink?" she cried.

We were struck dumb.

"You worthless, careless children!" she said. "I

go off for a brief errand of mercy and you—look what you do!" She was near tears. The fruit pie was ruined. It had slid into the standing water in the sink! Since the water was creamy green with slime and the home of numerous grateful bugs, this accident had not done the pie any good. For a while Maman couldn't even speak to us. She sent us to kneel with our faces against the wall of the front hallway, to think about our crimes.

"I want to know who did this!" she demanded. "And not a word among you to work up some awful lie about this! I will stand here and do the ironing and watch you until the grace of honesty returns to you again! You are French boys, and honor means something to you!" Then she heated the iron and pressed the clothes we needed for church. The smell of hot damp cotton filled the high-ceilinged hall in which we suffered together.

We waited in the hall and tried to be full of shame. But the devil gets into you at the worst possible moment. For some reason we fell prey to an attack of giggles. René especially. I remember his thin lips twisting, being bitten in an effort to keep in the bubbling giggles. "Hush," said Pierre, mortified, but René was hysterical, and hysteria is contagious. I tried to count the vases and jugs stored on the high shelf, to keep myself from giggling.

We had had the most serious adventure of our lives that afternoon! We had been visited by German soldiers and had smartly sent them away, and our wild mother didn't even know enough to be grateful to us! And we were not going to tell her, either.

But how *did* the pie fall into the outdoor sink?

To this day I don't know.

Many years have passed. Until Pierre died of cancer a few years ago, we would meet every five or six years, as many of the family as could. Our younger sisters Céleste and Agathe (who were born after the war), and René and his wife, and Pierre, and me and my wife and our Monique. After a few cognacs and a good cigar (among the men) we always began to talk about our childhood in France. Sooner or later the tale would be told of our first encounter with the German army. And around we would come to the question of who had bumped the pie into the sink.

"You did," René would accuse Pierre. "You were so nearsighted! And fiddling with your spectacles that day."

"I never did!" he always said, and turned to me. "It was you, Marcel! *You* were the clumsy one! *You* spilled the milk on the road, you fell out of that tree, you tipped the pie into the sink. You were hopelessly unbalanced in every limb. You were so fat then, a little ball of butter."

"It must've been René," I would answer. "It was he who was playing the marauding Hun. Remember, René? Brandishing that stick and darting about like one of the Three Musketeers with a bumblebee in your trousers."

But we never can know for certain.

"You're still lying!" we would say to each other. "You always were a good liar! You can tell the truth now—Maman is dead and won't punish us for it anymore!"

But none of us would ever confess.

What were we to do, kneeling there at the ages of eight, ten, and twelve, our knees hurting more horribly with every passing second? We went from shivery hysteria to righteous anger. We had bravely turned the entire German army from our mother's gate, and this was the thanks we got!

"I have many clothes to iron," Maman venomously reminded us. "And as we have nothing to eat tonight, it won't bother me to work until dark."

Since we were forbidden to talk to each other, I didn't yet know that not one of us *remembered* knocking the pie over. We all thought that one of us *was* holding out, waiting for a brother to confess and take the blame. But, I thought, why should *I* suffer the punishment if René or Pierre had actually done the crime? They *always* blamed me, just because I was the youngest.

I became stoical, an eight-year-old figure of stone. I would kneel there until I died. I had my pride. I hadn't spoiled the pie.

I didn't *think* I had.

We must have impressed Maman with our rigidity. She gave up that tactic and one by one called us into the parlor. One by one we were questioned about our afternoon. We didn't know what the others would say. But honor required that we suffer in silence. None of us mentioned the Germans. None of us confessed to pie smashing.

But when René was in the room with Maman the Grand Inquisitor, I whispered to Pierre, "I didn't do it; did you?"

"I didn't, and René said he didn't either!" said Pierre. Pierre was crying. Perhaps, four years older than I was, he understood just a bit better what it meant that the Germans had arrived. I didn't quite get it yet.

When it was growing dark—which means quite late in the evening, for this was June, when the days stay light forever—I finally had had enough. I had begun to feel rage at Maman for making Pierre cry. I began to sob and said, "I confess! I did it!"

I don't remember my punishment. As we snuggled together in our one big bed that night, however, my brothers gave me the supreme compliment. If I really *hadn't* been the culprit, then my lie was the best one of the day. Better even than René's deft lie about a sick grandmother in Chinon. I worried myself to sleep, grateful for the honor, wishing our father were home with us in these hard times. Maman would not be so strict if our father were around. He was strict enough for both of them.

I thought about him, off working somewhere. In the strange, illogical way that feelings have, I began to hate him a little bit for not staying here with us. Even though he was working to feed us. He misses us as much as we miss him, I told myself firmly. But I wasn't sure if that was true.

By the time we awoke the next morning and joined Maman for a few moments of prayers, the news had reached her. "My boys," she said quickly, "the Germans have arrived in Mont-Saint-Martin. Now the time for silliness and laziness is over." She lectured us for an hour on staying out of trouble. Keeping our mouths closed when any soldiers were around. Not wandering off. Not disobeying. "Your father would want you to be more brave and obedient than ever," she told us. "I know he would."

6

The Germans
Take Over

In time we learned that Paris had ground to a halt in the days before the invasion. But even as the Germans came in from the north, thousands of Parisians were fleeing to the south. On bicycles, in horsecarts, in their private automobiles if they were lucky enough to own them. The trains were unreliable.

When the German army marched in, France collapsed with a muffled thud in terror at the invasion. The country was divided. In the north the German army oversaw Occupied France—occupied by *them*, that is. Mont-Saint-Martin was in Occupied France.

Meanwhile, what was left of France's elected government retired to the town of Vichy, farther south. There the government presided over the part of the country that was not occupied by German forces; this section became known as Vichy France. Vichy France was organized by men—some old, some valiant, some stupid. But at its heart the Vichy government was an accomplice to the crime of invasion. It was like a person who, discovering he's being robbed one night, gets up to make tea for the burglars and sees that they're comfy and happy.

With the arrival of the German army, Paris began to work and live again. The *métro*—the underground train system—began to run again. Cinemas reopened. Paris did not burn, nor was it bombed. But the German secret police, the Gestapo, arrived in the City of Light on the same day as the German army, and the terrible consequences wouldn't be clear for some time yet.

In our lane, in our village, sunlight flooded the skies of childhood. What did we understand of the Nazis? Of collaboration with the enemy? Of the coming threat to French Jews? We Delarues had been Catholic for a thousand years; we hardly knew any Jews. The rabbi in the village and his circle of friends and followers—they weren't much to us. All that the invasion of Paris really meant to us was that Uncle Anton would soon be arriving with his friends.

And we grew used to the German presence. We didn't like it, but there it was. Our village was well situated on the north side of the Loire, between Tours and Neuillé-Pont-Pierre, just off the main road to Le Mans. There was a chateau on a man-made lake outside Mont-Saint-Martin, and that's where the soldiers and their commanding officers lived. They were separate from the battalions stationed in Tours, we guessed, because it was their job to comb the rich farmland for food for themselves and their companion soldiers all over France. The Germans used Mont-Saint-Martin as their headquarters and went out daily, to Saint-Antoine-du-Rocher, to Mettray, to Cerelles, to Beaumont-la-Ronce. Every evening they came back to the chateau. They slept under its fairy-tale conical towers. They cooked and ate its few swans. They scratched its parquet floors with their boots. What small reserves we had of our local wine they pissed away into the moat.

Yes, we grew used to the Germans as we waited for Uncle Anton. But it was more than a year before he finally showed up.

7
Uncle Anton

In the steamy early September of 1941, on a day in which late-summer butterflies staggered about in the winds, Uncle Anton and his friends finally arrived. They had got a train from the Gare d'Austerlitz in Paris to Tours, and with some difficulty had made their way to Mont-Saint-Martin. They stood at the garden gate for a minute, Uncle Anton calling for Maman. Though now we were a whole year older, and wiser, we boys were shyer of the new arrivals than we'd been of our German soldiers. Mirabeau yipped in excitement and danced on her back legs.

"The Delarue brothers," said Uncle Anton to

his companions. "Come unlatch the gate for us, Pierre."

"Maman," we called, "our uncle has come!"

He was a firm man with a barrel chest and arms like oak, which tapered into thin, papery-skinned fingers. He had a puckered face, as if he chewed on the insides of his cheeks. We knew him just well enough to grin and be silent. With Uncle Anton were his friend Madame Cauverian and her daughter, Miriam.

Madame Cauverian whistled involuntarily through a gap in her front teeth whenever she breathed hard. She breathed hard whenever she was anxious. She was anxious whenever she was awake, and during most of her sleep as well. No doubt she had grown used to the sound, but we found it annoying from first to last.

Miriam was about Pierre's age. She was an ugly thug of a child, with heavyset shoulders and an odd pelvis, which, we thought, might have been more at home on a zebra. (We weren't kind children.) I will tell you what we thought: We were ashamed to have her standing at our garden gate.

If Maman felt the same, we never knew it. She swept along the paving stones, lined at that time of the year with spiky-headed lavender, and she threw open the gate for them. In they came, with Mirabeau as suspicious as we were, yipping and yapping at any available heel.

We quickly realized that our guests weren't even French. They were French-speaking Belgians who had been living in Paris. We learned that Madame Cauverian was an artist, a painter, and also a Jew. (Uncle Anton moved in exotic circles, we decided.) She was very talented, we were told. We could see for ourselves that she was highly strung.

She wouldn't let the milk in the jug stand for a minute without re-covering it with its muslin cloth, weighted around the edge with green beads. As if a fly or a bee could land in it so quickly! She was constantly shutting windows and doors against the breezes. "Miriam is delicate; she will shiver," she said. Miriam looked about as delicate as a boulder. And Madame Cauverian insisted that the Germans were after the Jews. She and Miriam were fleeing across the Pyrenees to Spain, if they could get that far.

Madam Cauverian looked full of anger and sadness when she spoke. One morning over her tea she said, "Ghosts live in the soil. Do you know that, boys? Devils from the wicked dead arise through the ground, like fish through ocean waves, to plague us in our dreams. I can feel them nearby! Can you?"

René shrugged and looked at her with interest. It was hard for him not to ape her strong expressions.

Pierre, on the other hand, stared in amazement and belief.

She got up and closed another window, her tuneless whistle accompanying her wherever she went. "Miriam, you feel the spirits—you're a sensitive child, aren't you."

Miriam looked embarrassed at her mother. She said nothing. We felt a small pity for Miriam, to have a mother like that. A very small pity, and it didn't last.

"Why didn't you come a whole year ago, when Uncle Anton first wrote that Paris was falling?" asked René. Miriam rolled her eyes when her mother's back was turned.

But Madame Cauverian was firm. "The time wasn't right. All of Paris had been caught up in *la Grande Peur*, the Great Fear. I had to listen to my voices to tell when the hour had come to flee. It took me a whole year to sense that the coast was clear."

She listened to voices, like Joan of Arc!

"Is it like listening to the wireless?" René was always curious.

"René," said Pierre in a warning sort of voice. René wouldn't have heeded his older brother, but Maman was also shooting him threatening looks.

"We will stay a week. Of your kindness, we will rest, and then move on."

A whole week of the unwelcome guests! We would have to cut into seven portions food that had not been so ample when divided among only the four of us. But Maman said firmly, "We are honored."

But Maman thought Madame Cauverian was crazy too.

8

Jewish Guests

By now you should know of the fate of Europe's Jews during this period. It is a crucial fact in any history of the war years. No doubt your teacher has explained the meaning of the word *Holocaust*. Your teacher has pointed out *Auschwitz* and *Bergen-Belsen* on the map. The concentration camps, the death camps.

For part of the twentieth century, it was easier for Jews in France than in some countries—but this is all relative. Not so far away from where I grew up, in Chinon, Joan of Arc had met the Dauphin of France in the fifteenth century. How proud we were of living so near to that sacred spot! But just a hundred years earlier, all the Jews of the town were accused of poisoning the water supply and were burned alive.

For everyone who tells you stories of lion-hearted courage, of honor, of Liberty! Equality! Fraternity! there is someone still alive to tell a tale of helping the enemy, of blaming the weak. France is one of the few countries in Europe that, overrun by the Germans, caved in and cooperated.

"The Jews," Maman said once, "the Jews of France, they are different." She breathed in and out hard, pondering. She was, after all, a woman of no travel, little education. I believe she went to Paris only once in her life: Even to go to Orléans was a grand adventure for her. These were perilous times. It will be hard for you children to imagine a time before TV news. Now, the whole world rushes and gushes into your living room every night. Then, it was local gossip about the terrible things the Nazis were doing in Germany, in Poland, might do in Paris. "The Jews have strange prayers and eat strange food. They keep to themselves, and so they should." Maman was thoughtful. "But difference is not reason for such hatred," she continued. "If the Jews want to go away, to be safe, fine. Maybe it would be better for them, better for us. But they shouldn't be taken against their will."

However Maman felt about Jews in private, she was gracious and friendly to the Cauverians while they stayed with us. With our father away, Maman was the *chef de famille*, and we had to obey her.

Fortunately Maman did not force us boys to entertain Miriam. The girl sat in our parlor for hours on end, reading the works of Victor Hugo and biting her nails. Madame Cauverian fluttered and whistled from window to window, muttering to herself. If that's what it's like to be an artist, I thought, I'll never draw another picture again.

We thought that maybe Miriam was ashamed of her mother. Whenever her mother began to prophesy, Miriam looked down into her book. One day we even heard her mutter, "If you can read the future so well, why not tell me what's going to happen to Papa?" Madame Cauverian turned pale and left the room.

"Our father is gone too," said Pierre kindly, as if after a week Miriam might not have noticed.

"He's a pilot in Africa, flying supplies over the desert. He got shot down and is hiding in a pyramid," said René brightly.

"You're a liar," said Miriam matter-of-factly.

"Well, where's *your* father?" asked René without rancor, waiting for a good juicy fib in return.

"I don't know," said Miriam. She wouldn't say any more, and we wondered if her father was really off somewhere, in love with some other woman. If so, we didn't think Miriam was a very good liar. She looked flustered and pasty-faced. A dead giveaway.

"Our father trains wild camels in the moonlight," I said.

"He has a white stallion called Pride of the Sands," said René.

"He is building a bridge in Lorraine," said Pierre.

"You big liar!" we said, although that part was the truth. Still, we hated to lose face in front of Miriam, even if she was a girl.

We went into the kitchen.

"Do not mention our guests to the village,"

said Maman lightly to us. "The Cauverians do not wish to entertain while they are in Mont-Saint-Martin. They are merely resting."

"Nobody cares; nobody would want to come to see them," said René moodily.

We boys went out walking with Uncle Anton. The barley was high, roadside blackberries were ripening, the poplars blazed silvery green. Across the fields the blunted steeple of the church in the center of Mont-Saint-Martin looked golden-gray. "Do you like Madame Cauverian?" asked Uncle Anton.

"She is charming," said Pierre tonelessly. Not a very good lie, René and I thought. Who could believe it? Even Uncle Anton wasn't taken in.

"Charming?" he said, and laughed. "That's the last thing I'd have said."

Pierre, found out in his polite little lie, kicked a stone.

"She's most interesting," said René cunningly. "I never met a crazy woman before."

"She isn't crazy," said Uncle Anton. "She's intense."

"I'd like to see her in a circus with a man-eating tiger," said René. "I'd like to see the tiger tremble with fear!"

"Interesting to think about," said Uncle Anton.

"Do you love her?" I asked.

Uncle Anton laughed again. "I adore her," he said, "but not for a wife. I think René is right about her intimidating a tiger."

"Are you going to Spain with her?" said René.

But some German soldiers were walking by, and we had already fallen into the habit of not speaking in their presence. We didn't learn Uncle Anton's plans.

We stopped to buy some pills at the shop, I think because Madame Cauverian thought her precious Miriam looked peaked and in need of bolstering up. Old Madame Sevremont found the pills, counted them out twice, and wrapped them in a twist of newspaper. As Uncle Anton paid for them, Madame Sevremont remarked, "Are these for the woman and child staying at the Delarue home?"

"I do not know who wants them," said Uncle Anton. He changed the subject by complimenting Madame Sevremont's ugly gray hair, which was done up in a tortoiseshell comb from Brittany.

When we returned home, he said to Maman, "The old madame at the pharmacy has a sharp eye. She knows all!"

"And tells all," said Maman wearily. "She is troubled with a flapping tongue."

"Did you get the medicine?" asked Madame Cauverian, fluttering in. "Miriam is really feeling quite unwell Her forehead is so warm! Please, Anton, come and see for yourself."

We all trooped into the parlor. Miriam lay under a green blanket, looking glassy eyed and uncomfortable. "She's going in and out of a fever, poor thing," said her mother.

"She's finally found a way to escape her maman," said René under his breath. "Going into a feverish daze. That's clever."

But I felt a little sorry for her. Our maman said, "Maybe it's nerves, or lack of sunlight and proper nourishment. These are horrid times for children."

So Uncle Anton and the Cauverians stayed with us for much longer than a week. Madame Cauverian sat by Miriam, praying, cursing, reciting poems as if they were magic charms, singing in a ghastly breathy voice, and punctuating every offering with a little toot through her gapped teeth.

"Why don't you plug the chink with clay?" René asked her. René got smacked by Maman for unforgivable rudeness.

Our maman wiped Miriam's brow, heated saucers of milk to dip bread into, or brewed a broth of herbs and little else. There *was* little else.

Miriam recovered, but slowly.

Too slowly. When he came back from his stroll every day, Uncle Anton kept us abreast of the latest news. Before Miriam was feeling back to normal, he had observed that more German soldiers were arriving, almost daily. Maybe because it was harvest time.

"There are fears about harshness, about troubles," said Uncle Anton.

"What kind?" we asked, but Maman pursed her lips to keep her brother silent.

Uncle Anton did not always obey his sister. But with a glance at Miriam, languishing on the sofa, he sighed and said no more. And we boys had heard enough to be able to guess. We had heard the rumors that "actions" against the Jews in France had begun. In May and August both Polish-born Jews and French-born Jews were rounded up and sent to French detention camps. We weren't sure if this was just hysterical gossip.

But we didn't expect a search by German soldiers for Jews in Mont-Saint-Martin. We expected many other things, yes. We expected that brave, lonely Charles de Gaulle, the famous leader of Free France, would himself come striding from his exile in London, England, right into our own Mont-Saint-Martin, before we thought the Germans would bother us for Jews, foreign or otherwise.

Madame Cauverian grew more and more wild. She looked like a witch, with her ferocious black hair like spiders' webs spun into candy floss. We boys took to spending almost all our spare time fishing, or hiking with Mirabeau through the barley, or throwing stones at the birds, or stopping at the church to lodge a prayer for our absent father with the heavenly postal system. Anywhere but at home.

9
The Missing Tart

One day Maman decided to make some little berry tarts as a special treat, to celebrate Miriam's finally being able to sit up and eat real food again. We gathered some blackberries from their sunny homes. We got just enough. Maman rolled out the pastry, simmered precious sugar for a glaze, and managed to come up with seven glorious tarts. The berries were dark as ink and glistened under the sun. One whole tart *each*! We would not need to slice them into crumbling wedges! The miracle of a personal portion, intact and entire and private, filled us with joy.

But when the time came to serve the tarts, Maman found one was missing.

Oh! If we thought her anger over the pie in the sink was fierce, imagine this! To be shamed in front of guests!

I couldn't bear her to be ashamed of us. I was feeling very holy that day. I had been to church, and church always aroused in me hopes of goodness. I said, with a martyr's selflessness, "Oh, well, if one is missing, I will go without."

I set my face with humility, preparing to be admired for my Christian kindness.

"Guilty conscience!" said René. "*You* must've taken it!"

"How unlike you," said Pierre quietly. "Marcel, I'm so disappointed in you."

"How could you ruin our celebration for Miriam's return to health?" sighed and whistled Madame Cauverian.

"I didn't take it! I was just being good!" I said, but no one ever believed me. Except, I guess, the real thief, who never owned up. Possibly it was Mirabeau. But would she wolf down only one of seven pastry tarts cooling on a table or window ledge? It seems a bit unlikely.

10

Pierre's Accident

Not long after that, two terrible things happened.

The first was that Pierre spilled from our family bicycle and broke his leg. We had to straighten out the bicycle's bent wheel and send Uncle Anton on it to the nearest village boasting a true doctor. When the old man arrived in a private automobile, we were overcome with joy at the grandeur of it. An accident grants such dignity to ordinary people! The doctor set Pierre's leg and asked him what he'd been doing. "Trying to ride to Papa," said Pierre, in and out of consciousness. "I want Papa!"

We could never decide whether this qualified as a very good lie or not. The doctor seemed to believe him.

The doctor looked at Miriam, too, and afterward he went into a room with Maman, Uncle Anton, and Madame Cauverian. René and I could hear the sound of serious voices, muffled in alarm. René crept close and listened. He flung himself away and busied himself with an imaginary stone in his shoe as they came out, looking grim. "The doctor says there's going to be harder times for Jews in France," René told me later. "In Vichy France there was a decree calling for the rounding up of all foreign Jews."

"We're Occupied France, so who cares?" I said. I was now almost ten, and I pretended to know a lot more than I really did.

"But he says in *Paris* last year the Germans ordered a census of all Jews. Perhaps the Nazis will round them *all* up and take them away, he says."

"Take them where?" I asked.

René didn't know.

"You mean Miriam and Madame Cauverian?"

"Maybe," he said.

"At least we'll have more to eat then," I said, still smarting from the unjust accusations made about the blackberry tart.

• • •

The second terrible thing that happened was that Mirabeau disappeared.

Mirabeau had never taken to Madame Cauverian. The dog liked her even less than we did. Perhaps that hissing sound in Madame Cauverian's dentures alarmed Mirabeau. She would growl in a low, throaty way and stand with head down and legs planted apart. She would glare menacingly toward wherever Madame Cauverian was sitting, beset by her terrible prophetic dreams. Mirabeau was not making Madame Cauverian's unpleasant autumn any nicer.

So at first we wept when one day our dog didn't show up. Then we wept harder on the second and third days, after fruitless searches and plaintive cries for "Mirabeau! Mirabeau!" We asked all the neighbors, we plastered the village with home-made signs announcing her disappearance.

Coming back from yet another useless search for her, I began to sulk in a dark anger. I said to my brothers, "I bet that Madame Cauverian is a witch, and she has put a spell on the dog."

"Well, she really looks like a witch," said René, and did a hobbling imitation.

"Don't be ridiculous, René," said Pierre. "She is a perfectly decent person."

"You're so trusting; that's because you're so dim and dull," said René meanly. "You would trust a devil if he smiled at you."

Pierre was always hurt when we made fun of his slow, deliberate way of thinking and doing things. He knew he wasn't very bright.

"Maybe Madame Cauverian even had Mirabeau killed," I went on mercilessly.

René and I dropped nasty hints in the direction of Miriam and her mother. But they acted as innocent as mice. "When are they going to leave?" we began to complain to Maman. "Nothing's the same with them around."

"Nothing is the same," Maman agreed heavily, "but it isn't them. It's France."

Time dragged on. Miriam was still too sick to travel. We murmured brief hellos and avoided her most of the time. I didn't like her, but I didn't suspect *her* of Mirabeau's demise.

11
A Day Out

One day Maman woke us with a surprise. "Hurry. I'm sending you both to Monsieur Nicodeme's farmhouse for some honey," she said to René and me. "Can you remember the way, René? Pierre is still too stiff on his bad leg to show you."

"I can remember," lied René neatly. "Of course I can."

We didn't question the haste with which we were spruced up for a day out, nor the sudden liberty sprung on us. Maman gave us a small loaf of bread, half a tin of meat paste, two hard-boiled eggs, and some grapes. She kissed us fiercely. She told us to take the high road out of town and cut through the pear orchards of the convent to reach the dirt track to Monsieur Nicodeme's farm. She handed us an envelope for Monsieur Nicodeme.

It was a long walk. To our surprise we didn't get lost. We griped and gossiped and finished our lunch fifteen minutes after we'd left our garden gate. René got stung by a bee. I threw a stone at a soldier, but it fell short. We discussed how much we missed our father. We admitted wishing that the German soldier would come looking for Maman again. We didn't *like* the army being around Mont-Saint-Martin, but we had begun to feel a special fondness for "our" soldier. He hadn't been scary at all. Very polite. Whenever we had seen him around the village, he had smiled at us, and although we gallantly stared back stony faced, we were secretly pleased at his remembering us.

Monsieur Nicodeme gave us the honey and opened the envelope that Maman had sent him a note in. Not until later did I realize that Maman must have asked him to keep us safely on his farm for the entire day.

Monsieur Nicodeme sighed. He took us for a ride on his donkey cart and showed us how he was repairing his barn. We went up to an old three-sided shed at the top of a high field, and he told us an unconvincing ghost story about a phantom goat. He let us feed the hens. He insisted we swim in the spring pool, which was freezing at this time of the year. His wife was off visiting her sister and he was lonely, he said.

Charity permitted us to hang around and keep him company. We told him Pierre had broken his leg and had it chopped off. That's why he wasn't with us. We told him our father had been kidnapped by the Nazis and was in prison in Germany. We told him Mirabeau had drowned while trying to save a baby drifting down the Loire in a wicker basket. Monsieur Nicodeme looked very sad to hear this and kept shaking his head, saying, "Boys, boys, what a life you lead."

We had a great day. We gobbled up blackberries. We climbed in the apple trees. We finally trudged home, full of stories to tell Pierre.

12

The Roundup

Once home, we found out that we had missed the central event of the war in Mont-Saint-Martin.

Perhaps old Madame Sevremont had gabbled too loudly in the presence of German soldiers, complaining of the strange requests of her Polish customers, how hard a time she had understanding them.

The Germans had rounded up all the foreigners suspected of being Jewish. They had taken the rabbi first, and his noisy terrified friends. The soldiers had taken them to the *mairie,* the mayor's office, and asked each one questions. Most of them had been herded into trucks and driven to Tours, I guess. It had been swift, efficient, silent, and terrible. We would not know until many years later that the rabbi had been the real target. He had had a political past and was worthy, apparently, of being tracked down even to the small village of Mont-Saint-Martin.

Whatever the reasons, René and I had missed it all.

Maman had had word from the doctor in the neighboring village that the roundup was predicted. She had meant to spare us the awful sight of it.

But she had also spared us witnessing the departure of our deranged Madame Cauverian and her huge, miserable daughter, Miriam.

"Gone *where*?" demanded René. "First Papa leaves, then Mirabeau gets lost, now the Cauverian family! Why didn't they wait till we got back to say good-bye?"

"They couldn't wait," said Maman, with a terrible heaviness in her voice.

"Don't carry on so," said Uncle Anton to René and me. "You didn't really enjoy having them here very much."

"Well, that's no excuse for rudeness," said René, pouting.

Pierre lay on the sofa with his face toward the wall. He wasn't asleep, but he wouldn't speak to us. René gave his injured leg a fierce punch when Maman wasn't looking.

The truth was, we felt guilty. We'd been making fun of Madame Cauverian. We had aped her behind her back. All those dire predictions! She had seen angels of death hidden inside mirrors! She had read curses in how onion peels fell on the table! She'd gone around and around in the same orbit. By now René had perfected a wicked imitation of her, complete with the miniature wind puffing out the side of his mouth.

And Miriam, the poor sick thing. We should have been nicer to her. We'd been very callous. We felt terrible.

Uncle Anton made us airplanes out of old newspapers, but we didn't care to play with them. All the pleasures of our lies at Monsieur Nicodeme's farm fell away. We ate our supper in silence, nothing but a bowl of fish-head soup, a little red wine with water in it, a crust of bread. We wanted to know if *our* soldier had in fact come to the house to take away Madame Cauverian and Miriam. But Uncle Anton didn't know we *had* a soldier called "our" soldier, and how could we admit it now?

Pierre, because of his bad leg, no longer slept in the same bed with us. He had taken to sleeping on a mattress on a floor in the front hallway. So we couldn't whisper our questions to him that night. When finally we did, a day or two later, he merely answered, "Shut up about it, will you." He looked so unhappily at us that we knew our worst fears were well founded.

13
Maman
Makes a Scene

A few days later, maybe a week or two, Uncle Anton, Maman, René, and I set out one afternoon to the shop. We stopped outside for a while, while Maman and Uncle Anton had a long meandering conversation of the sort that bores children. A couple of German soldiers came along on a stroll and stopped in the shop for something. Maman threw her shoulders back and said to us, "Come now, my little chickens. Be good now." We all went through the open doorway and into the shadowy gloom inside the shop.

Madame Sevremont was measuring some powder on a scale. Soldiers made her nervous, and she had to start over several times. "Good day, Madame Sevremont," said Maman loudly. "It is I, Madame Delarue, with my brother and my sons."

"Yes, yes, in a minute. I am busy," said Madame Sevremont.

"Oh, I did not see these customers," said Maman in a voice no one could help hearing every syllable of. The soldiers were standing only a foot away.

"Please, Bernadette," said Uncle Anton. "Do not become excited."

"I am *not excited*," said Maman in a testy voice, not like herself. René and I gripped each other's hands. "I observe we are sharing the pharmacy with German soldiers who abduct stateless guests of France." She meant the foreign Jews.

"Maman," said René, pulling at her apron, while I, coward that I was, wet my underclothes.

"You should be ashamed," said Maman distinctly, each word pushed a little bit away from the next, as if to make her French as clear as possible to German ears. "A mother and her daughter. So what if they were Jews! Whatever had they done to you?"

"Maman, let's go home," said René. We were both crying.

"Bernadette, have you lost your senses?" said Uncle Anton. "Officers, please, the strain has been too great. Her husband, a builder, is serving Germany in Lorraine. She is distraught. I must go back to Paris, and it is hard for her to be a woman alone in these times."

"Do not talk over my head at these men," snapped Maman to her brother.

"You will forgive her." Uncle Anton winked at the soldiers. "You understand women. You are men of the world."

The soldiers nodded courteously to my uncle and ignored my mother. "*I* will not forgive *you*," said Maman. With deliberate lack of speed she stood her ground. She made an unusual face. Before we knew what was happening, she had spit on the terra-cotta floor at the boots of the German soldiers.

Madame Sevremont wailed and knocked the powder on the counter. "Good afternoon, Madame Sevremont," said Maman proudly. She stalked away. Her head wasn't held high; in fact she was hunched over as if she were having trouble breathing properly. "Don't squeeze my hand so tightly!" complained René through his tears.

"Well done, well done," muttered Uncle Anton all the way home. "Bernadette, I am in awe! Well done."

Maman just shook her head and said, "These times! Who can believe these strange times we are living in!"

René and I didn't know what to think about all this. They certainly were strange times, that could make our timid mother speak so tauntingly to a German soldier. How had she dared to lash out at a German soldier? Yes, Maman was strong and brave—but usually she was also sensible. It gave me a deep, cold pit in my stomach, to think how a person you knew so well could change right before your eyes.

14

The Funeral

Not long after that, Uncle Anton returned to Paris. Mirabeau still had not shown up, so we held a little funeral service for her in the garden. The time of apples had come and gone, the time of pears, of warmth. The fall thickened and chilled into a rainy winter. We did not hear from our father. We took turns telling of the accomplishments of Mirabeau to all mourners, who included a few of our childhood friends.

"She was a good dog. She was brave and bit Germans hard," said René. Mirabeau had actually wagged her tail fiercely at the sound of German boots on stone.

"She was a kind dog and loved one and all,"

said Pierre, omitting Mirabeau's firm opinions about Madame Cauverian.

"She was a saint and saved a baby from a burning building once," I said, weeping with passion over the thought of it, how brave Mirabeau would have been had she ever had the chance.

We prayed to the Virgin that Mirabeau be allowed into heaven so that she could be there, wagging her tail at the gates, when we got there.

We were sorry the Germans had taken Madame Cauverian and Miriam. We thought they might have enjoyed this little spectacle of grief. Anyway, they probably would have enjoyed the jars of tomatoes we started opening. It was always a treat to have summer garden crops in the winter. As it happened, we didn't seem to have that much more to eat now that the Cauverians were gone, the only small benefit to have been expected in such a sorry story.

15
Monsieur Soldier

Rain, fog, once in a while some snow. After the harvest some of the German soldiers went elsewhere for the winter, but a small number of them stayed on in the chateau of Mont-Saint-Martin. Among the skeleton crew was our own soldier, whom by now we had taken to greeting with smileless, sideways nods of recognition. Very much as grown-ups greet each other—formally, coolly. Most of our school friends treated the soldiers with an admirable theatrical haughtiness, or else they went out of their way to avoid them. But we had a nameless bond with our soldier, whom we had nicknamed "Monsieur Soldier."

One day I had taken our family bicycle into the

village. I ran into Monsieur Soldier in the doorway of the church. I was stopping to go to confession. I had become more strict with myself and felt the need to admit my lies to the priest. This didn't stop my lying. In a pleasant way I always felt eager to get back to lying again after the balm of forgiveness and the payment of penance.

"I didn't know you went to church!" I blurted out.

"I didn't know you did," he answered, in that strange slipped-gear accent. We French of Touraine prided ourselves on having the best accent in France and scorned even Parisians. . . . What was I doing being so gracious toward someone who mangled our silky language, wrinkled it into raw pulp?

"Are you a Catholic?" I asked, amazed at my boldness. What stories to tell René and Pierre tonight!

"No," he said. "I don't believe in God right now."

I looked shocked.

"I will again one day," he said. "It is hard to believe in God during the war."

"Why did you come to take away our friends?" I asked.

"Your friends the chickens?" he said, for that had happened once.

"No, the Jewish friends from Paris and Belgium. The Cauverians."

"I didn't do that," he answered. "It will be my fellow soldiers you must ask, I suppose."

I felt very relieved. It made the distant unlikely affection we had for him less terrible. "You look a little bit like my father," I said to him.

"And you," he said, "you do not look like my brother at all. He is much handsomer than you! But you remind me how much I miss him. He is in Düsseldorf. His name is Karl."

"Oh," I said. I didn't mind reminding him of Karl.

Along the cobblestones in her good church shoes came Madame Sevremont, the pharmacy lady. Poor thing, she was tormented by recent accusations that her wagging tongue had put the Germans on to food supplies hidden in farmhouses around about. She tried with a constant lack of success not to speak in the presence of soldiers. But she couldn't help observing to our soldier in passing, "The church is no place for the likes of you. Mercy on us all."

I felt I shouldn't be seen chatting to Monsieur Soldier, or Madame Sevremont would tell the world. So I said good-bye and slipped in through the small door cut neatly right into the skin of the larger door. Nowadays they cut cat flaps and doggie doors into human doors—it was like that. This was a human door hinged into a broader door that was large enough for three harnessed horses prancing abreast.

In the cool forgiveness of the church I played my holy games. You must understand about churches in France. The cathedrals are like great stone ships sailing through the green fields and endless decades. What Shakespeare is to the English language, what Mozart arias are to vocal music, the French cathedrals are to church buildings. The expression of genius, an idea perfectly realized. The smaller churches of France are like lifeboats sent out from the master cathedrals. They each have their own character. They each are loved for their stone habits and their patchy renovations and their unique shabbiness.

The church in Mont-Saint-Martin—you can still see it, for all I know—was a pretty plain affair. But it had one glory that it had copied from the cathedral at Chartres: It had the pattern of a maze set in different-colored paving stones in the floor just inside the main entrance. There were superstitions about the maze: It confounded the devil, for one. But we had our own private family rituals around the maze. To approach the altar in prayer after having been lying vigorously all week, we had to walk along the path of the maze while holding our breath. This was very hard to do, and we never made it, but it was the effort that counted. As we got older, we would be able to hold our breath longer, and one day we would be successful.

On this day I followed the path of the maze to the center, to stand on a mosaic of the Holy Ghost. I watched Madame Sevremont bob her head and kneel with difficulty. She sank her face into her hands. I did not think she was clever enough to commit any serious and interesting sins. But I was beginning to feel uneasy about having had a conversation with Monsieur Soldier. My prayers were more heartfelt than usual that afternoon.

16
Pierre
Is Reformed

It was some time in the winter of 1941–42 that Pierre began to stop lying.

"Why?" said René. It was raining and we were trying, without success, to remember how Uncle Anton had folded newspapers into airplanes.

"Because it's wrong," he said.

"Well," said René, "of course it is, but if nobody's hurt, what's the problem?"

"It is harder to tell the truth than to lie," said Pierre slowly. "I like to do the thing that is harder."

"You're crazy."

"I like myself better if I make myself be the way I *want* to be," said Pierre.

"You're just giving up. You never *were* a good

81

liar," said René. "What's hard for you is lying. *That's* the thing you should practice."

I didn't like to see my big brothers fighting. "Let's steal some bread from the kitchen," I said.

"No," said Pierre.

"Oh, now you've become holy-holy. How ridiculous!" said René.

"Will you close your mouth?" said Pierre. "There's a war going on. We shouldn't make things any harder."

"But I'm hungry," I said. "Just some bread, what's so bad about that?"

"No," said Pierre. "No more stealing food."

"You're no fun—you're becoming a crabby grown-up," I said.

"Oh, I know why you've been such a sour-puss!" said René suddenly. "Pierre, you're in love with Miriam Cauverian! And you miss her madly! Why didn't I work it out before?"

"You're crazy," said Pierre, and threw a pillow at René.

We began to chant. "Pierre and Miriam, Miriam and Pierre!"

Pierre was so enraged that he launched himself

off the sofa at us. But his mended leg was still giving him trouble, so he couldn't wring our necks as he would have liked. We hopped, squealing with glee, away from him, and we teased him mercilessly for weeks afterward.

17
Nightmares
and Consolations

For a time I had nightmares. I kept dreaming about our father. As the Germans had come to take Madame Cauverian and Miriam away, had they also taken our father? Why wasn't he with us? Maybe our lie about him was true. Maybe he *was* in a prison in Germany. I dreamed he would come home but hide from us. Because he didn't love us. That he would be so thin, he could fit in the shallow cupboards, or drift like smoke in between the floorboards. I dreamed that the house was a maze, and Papa had come home and was keeping away from us inside. I would wake up crying. Maman always seemed to be awake, coming with a lantern. We did have electricity, but she was afraid the overhead light would wake my brothers.

"I want Papa," I would cry, suddenly the baby of the family again and unashamed to be lonely for him.

"You mustn't cry," said Maman.

"But I keep dreaming he's coming back!" I said. "I keep dreaming he's moving around us like a ghost. Is he dead?"

"How could a dead person write us the letter we got last week?" said Maman.

"I don't know," I wailed. "Maybe dead people are good letter writers."

"You're being silly."

"I hate him," I'd say, even as I was missing him. "It's not fair."

"It's the war," Maman explained. Then she would sing songs to me until I fell asleep.

I never told Pierre or René about my dreams. Often I couldn't remember them the next day. One night I dreamed Miriam Cauverian came to my bedside instead of Maman, and read to me from Victor Hugo. I didn't tell Pierre or René that dream because I didn't want them making fun of me! I was embarrassed, having a dream about a girl.

One afternoon when I was alone in the house, I looked down into the musty cellar where precious few jars of tomatoes and green beans stood randomly on the shelves. I thought I might find Papa there. But there was no one, just a spider on a shelf, crumpled up like the dead head of a flower.

18

Resistance

Time passed. I will be honest and say I didn't notice much difference, month by month. But around me the ship of History was letting out her sails, pivoting in the winds. From abroad General Charles de Gaulle was mounting a campaign to recapture France. He called for resistance of the Nazis by all French citizens. At the same time Hitler's army was strengthening its hold on France. For adults life was filled with terror. You couldn't know which of your neighbors might be informing the German police, or the local *gendarmes*, or the Milice, the paramilitary band of Fascist Frenchmen. (Some French *did* collaborate with invading Germans to save their skins.) You couldn't know which of your neighbors might be involved secretly in the Resistance. (Some French, out of contempt for German force, bravely fought in the Resistance.) Many more of the French people, my family among them, appeared merely to live out the war hoping to squeak through unnoticed and unharmed.

Tiny and backwater though Mont-Saint-Martin was, a small local Resistance movement had come into being. If I ever knew any details of the espionage against our German occupiers, I have forgotten them. I remember, though, that one of our local priests was arrested. I think he had been caught giving sanctuary to a British pilot (who'd been shot down in the north and was slowly making his way via safe houses to the Mediterranean port of Marseilles, where a system for smuggling people out of France had been set up). The pilot was shot to death by our own *gendarmes* in the Place du 11 Novembre. (The name of our town square honored the date of liberation from the Germans after World War I.) Maman wouldn't let us go and watch it. I don't know what happened to the priest. What I *did* see, a day or two later, was horrific in a different way.

It was Sunday, and as a family we were making our way to Mass.

When we got to the church, we joined the throng in the cobblestoned street outside, gaping at what we saw.

A German tank—I think it was a Panzer Mark II—had been driven across the low threshold of our church. It had smashed apart like matchsticks the two large front doors of the building. The ancient iron hinges were torn from the stone; the ancient wood lay in splinters every which way. The tank had scraped against the stone on either side of the doorway (the scrapes would be visible to this day) and then rolled into the back of the church.

It sat squarely on the stone maze, like a huge pagan turtle, the barrel of its gun pointing toward the altar. Around it the colored sluices of the few stained-glass windows let in floods of red and blue and green and golden light. The tank all but covered the maze. The monsignor was weeping and pushing back at the tank with his shoulder, though he might as well have been pushing at the Alps for all the effect he had.

The men in the village were frightened to show a reaction, but I suppose somebody must have gone to the police. Someone must have said: Yes, we get the message. Resistance will be squashed wherever it crops up, even in the sanctuary. We understand what the Germans are saying.

But we will not tolerate the tank in our church.

They got it out of there, our village men. I don't know if someone climbed in it and shifted its gears or if it was sheer brawn. But in their good white Sunday shirts, with their soapy necks and Sunday glistening shaved chins, the men of Mont-Saint-Martin got their shoulders against the tank and shoved against it. Some of the women were weeping, some praying aloud to the Virgin, and one or two putting their own Sunday-scrubbed hands on the shoulders of the men.

"Where is our father?" I said. "He should be here."

"Shh, don't say that," said Maman, with a

strong feeling of agreement in her voice, or so I thought.

Pierre heard me, and in his glinting spectacles he went up to the tank too. Limping along on the leg that would never completely heal, a narrow bewildered boy among the men, pushing as hard as he could. He was so good to me.

19
Silenced!

As spring meandered in, things became more chilly in town. I mean chilly as to people's moods, people's tendency to clam up about anything important. When the world was in the lush flowering of May 1942, we learned about the decree, several months earlier, that required Jews to wear the yellow Star of David armbands. French Jews, the gossip went, would be safe; but those foreign ones, the ones who practiced the arcane rituals, who wore the side curls, who spoke Yiddish, the ones from the misbegotten back alleys of Middle Europe—they might not be safe. From the wealthier of the foreign Jews property was being taken. The abduction of our rabbi and his congregation in Mont-Saint-Martin had been small stuff compared to this. There were rumors of murder.

Madame Cauverian had been right to be so frantic.

A thorough lunatic about some things, she had seen the German threat to the Jews exactly for what it was. One evening, when I wanted to mention my grief at what had happened to the Cauverians, both Maman and Pierre turned to me and said, "Hush! We don't even speak of them now. It is as if they were never here! Do you know what might happen to us if anyone suspected we had had Jews as guests? They might come and search for more, and make no end of trouble for us."

I resented that Pierre now considered himself the man of the family and talked to me in that tone of voice. I sulked. "We could simply lie— we're good at that. It's the family talent," I muttered. Maman looked sharply at me, and I waited for her to punish me for even suggesting that we do something so wrong. But she held her tongue.

"*L'air du temps*, Marcel," she said simply, and put her lips together in a theatrical way. She meant: In the spirit of these times, my boy, we keep our mouths closed.

20

Dangerous Friends

"**C**ome on," I said to René one day, when beautiful late-spring weather was at its height and the whole world was frilly and aromatic with white blossoms. "Let's take the bicycle and go fishing."

We had our favorite spot for fishing. It was only a short way out of town, where a nameless stream broadened and flowed into the Choisille, our own river, which joined the Loire farther down. A pretty accident of geography had arranged for us a grassy tongue of land, flanked by the river on one side and the stream converging from the other. There was a tree, perhaps a water hickory. Dogs often came to this vantage point and stood sniffing the wind and looking for fish. Kids came too, and sometimes drunks.

We called this place the *fleur-de-lis*, because it tapered like the top central petal of France's royal emblem. Here we were used to privacy. We made silly jokes, we complained, sometimes we practiced swearing since no adults were around. We were alone and having little luck, just pulling from the water small brown fish hardly bigger than a baby's fingers. We threw them back, disgusted. Sometime during the afternoon Monsieur Soldier wandered along.

We weren't accustomed to being visited by German soldiers. However, since the *fleur-de-lis* had never been visited by old Madame Sevremont, or most others of the local grown-ups either, René and I felt as if we didn't need to be so carefully unfriendly this time. We said "Hello" to our soldier.

He chatted with us awhile and expressed disappointment over our catch. "My younger brother Karl can catch better fish than that," he said.

"You have fish in the streets of Düsseldorf?" I asked.

"Hah!" He laughed. "No, but our grandfather has a farm in Bavaria, loveliest of countries. We fish there all the time and are better than you. German fish are stout and good, not like these slender pale threads you pull out of the water."

He showed us a few fishing tricks we didn't know. He showed us how to cast, even with our rustic rods, so that the fishing line went farther out than three feet. He suggested we whisper so the fish wouldn't be scared off. We began to whisper.

It's funny when you whisper. Whether you mean to or not, you feel as if you're saying something important. You feel closer to the listener. You have to lean closer. René and I both leaned closer to Monsieur Soldier.

We told him our name for him, sitting up next to him. His arms went out like wings, and each of us was inside next to his shoulder, smelling his grown-up male sweat in his uniform. He laughed. "Why couldn't you call me Monsieur Kommandant! Or Monsieur Führer! You insult me!" he said.

He never did tell us his real name.

And then began a beautiful summer. I have forgotten what distinguished each time we met from the others. They are a pleasant blur, a blur featuring good weather, laughs and ticklings, jokes and stolen food to share (Monsieur Soldier was a rogue like us, and could steal better treats from the commissary than we could from our larder or pantry). I remember our soldier taking off his uniform and showing us how to dive. He was a good-looking man. As the French say sometimes, he was a man who fitted his skin well.

René and I would ride home on our single bicycle. We coasted through the shadowy avenue of hollow trees, whose branches had been clipped some years back so that the new limbs sprang straight up, like candles on the arms of a living candelabra. Each time, I worried about what we would say when we got home.

But René lied better each time. We never mentioned the ripening friendship with our soldier. Not even to Pierre, who was growing gloomier and less fun and more grown-up with every passing week. We knew that it could cause problems, and we felt we already had more than enough problems.

• • •

And then, because things like this end (they have to), it all came crashing down. Well, I should rewrite that line. *I* came crashing down—literally. And I brought the summer idyll down with me.

We had been joking over what a bad fisherman I was, and for a lark I climbed out onto one of the branches of the hickory tree. I was saying that I would be farther out from the bank than they would, and could pitch my line farther. I would get better fish than they did. I didn't really expect to. It was a joke taken too far, but nobody minded. We all kept giggling.

And we didn't worry that I might fall in. I could swim. Half the fun about playing near water is falling in, anyway.

But I wasn't called Fat Marcel for nothing. The branch cracked under my weight and sent me tumbling and shrieking into the water just off the *fleur-de-lis*. Alas, I didn't let go of the stake I was using as a fishing pole. Somehow it fell into the water ahead of me and drove into the mud at the bottom of the river. When I fell, I landed on it and knocked out some teeth and ripped open my bottom lip.

Monsieur Soldier was up in an instant and hurtling himself, fully clothed, into the water. He picked me up—I was screaming torture and agony—and slogged his way back to the shore. He bound up the bottom of my face in my shirt, to keep what was left of my lip more or less in place. Then he began to carry me home.

I tried to say that I could walk by myself. I wasn't a baby—by now I was ten years old! But I couldn't speak with my mouth bandaged up. And René had gone white with fear. He just ran alongside the long strides of Monsieur Soldier, pushing our bicycle and panting to keep up. I'm sure he was trying to make up a good lie as to what we were doing and how I had split my face in two.

When we got close to the house, René finally said, "This is close enough. Thank you very much. I will bring my brother into the house."

"Don't be silly. You can't carry him," said Monsieur Soldier.

"I insist," said René firmly.

"Nonsense," said our soldier, and he took me into the garden. He rapped on our kitchen door and opened it, calling out in his ugly French,

"Hello, hello to the mother of Marcel, please!"

Maman came to the doorway from the front room, and she did not speak to our soldier. She took me out of his arms and laid me on the kitchen table as if I were a chicken to be plucked and quartered. Pierre hobbled his way into the kitchen and turned his own shade of pale gray. "What have you done to our Marcel?" he asked.

"Pierre, no," said Maman.

"What have you done?" he asked again, louder, being the man in the house with our father still far away.

"I have brought him home," said our soldier. "He is hurt."

"How did he get hurt?" asked Pierre.

"We were riding our bicycle together, Marcel and I," said René quickly, "up near where the patisserie used to be before it closed and all the pastries in the window got dusty. Where Sérafine the piano teacher has her lessons, that corner. Some stupid child threw a stone for fun, and it hit Marcel in the face. I skidded when he screamed! Oh, it was awful. Down by the war memorial this soldier was standing, and he saw me crash into the wall—"

"What are you saying?" said our soldier. "The young boy fell out of a tree into the water and onto his fishing pole. We were fishing at the place you call the *fleur-de-lis*, the same place we have fished all summer. Madame, you must look quickly at his lip and his teeth. I understand you have some medical training."

Maman was undoing my shirt from around my chin, into which a gorgeous amount of blood had soaked. I was particularly proud of that blood. She poked my jaw, moved my lip this way and that, looking. "All summer long?" she said faintly. "Fishing together all summer long?"

"You do not know of this?" said our soldier.

"A bicycle accident, René?" said Maman with a raised eyebrow.

"Oh, help," said René, and he sat down with his face in his hands.

I looked from one face to the other. It is hard to explain what I felt. On the one hand I was proud of the extended lie—we boys had kept our soldier a secret since the day he had first showed up at the garden gate with his sick companion. And I had grown fond of him. I wanted Maman to thank him most kindly for taking care of me. I wanted her to realize that not all the soldiers were bad. I wanted her to see how kind he had been to me. I was still thinking, even now, that perhaps he would become a regular visitor to our household.

"Pierre," said Maman, "get the kind officer a glass of wine."

But her voice did not say *Welcome*. Her voice did not say *Thank you*. It said *Just this and no more*. I knew my strong-willed mother well enough to hear her opinions coming loudly and strongly through her politeness. Pierre, with a shaking hand, poured out a glass of red wine. He did not put any water in it. He handed it to our soldier without looking at him. A little wine spilled over the edge and ran onto Pierre's hand, on the stretchy part between thumb and fingers. He mouthed his hand dry like a dog licking itself, almost absent-mindedly.

"My sons do not go fishing with soldiers of any army," said Maman as she began to look more deeply into my mouth and to feel my teeth. "I hope you hear me and understand what I am saying. They are boys and you are a man. They do not understand the world. It is not correct. I will not have it."

"I did not know there was any deception involved, Madame," said Monsieur Soldier stiffly. He took a sip of the wine and set it down unfinished. "I will leave if I can be of no further help."

"You are wet and wrinkled and muddy," said Maman. "But it cannot be helped. I must look after my boy. You will be taken care of at your garrison?"

"Of course."

"Please," said Maman, as if struggling with herself. "Please do not return to see how the boy is doing. He will recover nicely. It is not a major wound. I thank you for treating the situation seriously."

"You are welcome."

"We can *not* be friends," said Maman. "None of us. It is too hard. You must understand this."

"Good afternoon," said our soldier. He looked at me. I am afraid to say that I was crying, although whether it was pain from the wound or grief at the terrible way things were turning out I do not know. "You will be a good fisherman yet," said

Monsieur Soldier. "But you'll never be as good as Karl."

I didn't move. René, however, leaped up and threw his arms around our soldier and kissed the buttons on his coat. I didn't know until that moment that René had liked him as much as I had. I was jealous of René's bravery and also his mobility; I was still pinned down to the table by Maman's capable hands.

"I will see you to the gate," said Pierre primly. In his spectacles he looked like a miniature diplomat or a minor lawyer. Out of the door went our soldier. Pierre escorted him to the street, then came back and closed the door firmly, locking it with a loud, ugly sound.

"Why are you so hateful?" I said, but no one could understand what I was saying.

21

The Great Lie

Maman did not speak to me or René for several hours, except to ask me did this hurt, did that. There was no way I could get to see a dentist until the following week, so Maman pressed my jaw with a cold cloth to keep the swelling down. René tried to say something several times, but Maman said, "Do not speak to me, René, or I will hit you harder than you think I can."

Even Pierre, now that his duty being man of the house was done, looked worried.

Maman collected fresh carrots and greens from the garden. She made a salad, and she brought out a small loaf of bread and some sausage for supper. She cut two apples into pieces and arranged them on a plate. She set all the food on the table.

Then she sat down and did not move.

"Are we going to eat?" asked René when the four of us had sat for an hour, brooding, me with a throbbing jaw. The white flesh of the apples had turned brownish.

Maman did not answer. She sighed several times and turned her apron up into her hands. She picked at where dried bread dough had caught in floury clumps on the fabric, and flicked off the bits onto the floor. Only once in the long dusk did she speak. "What would your father think of you?" she said, as if she were really wondering, not entirely sure herself.

The dusk became night. At last, when René and I were ready to drop into sleep where we sat, Maman arose. She drew the curtains and lit a candle. She then said, "Pierre. It is time."

Pierre got up and looked at her. "Maman, are you sure?"

She did not answer. She wasn't sure. "Go ahead," she said.

Pierre looked scathingly at René and me. He went into the front hall and climbed up the stepladder to the high shelf where Maman kept her earthenware jugs and vases and the three pieces of fine crystal she and our father had received for wedding presents. With his bad leg it took Pierre some time, up and down the ladder, to clear the shelf of its wares. Maman did not get up to help, nor did she tell René or me to go to Pierre's aid. So we sat there, completely mystified.

When the shelf was bare, Pierre climbed the stepladder again. He rapped twice against the ceiling, and then he made his way down the ladder.

There was the sound of movement above.

"Papa?" said René.

I could not speak, not with my sore lip and jaw, not with my heart in my mouth.

I hadn't known there was a crawl space over that part of the house. Over the bedrooms we had the small attic in which we stored trunks and old clothes and broken furniture. When we were very little, we used to play there on rainy afternoons in the summer. But the house was lower on the side where the passageway led from the front door to the other rooms. It didn't rise two flights. It wasn't supposed to have a crawl space!

But two boards from the ceiling were being lifted away by hands I couldn't see.

And two feet came down gingerly, finding the top step of the ladder and proceeding at a slow pace toward the floor.

Miriam Cauverian came into view.

She was no longer fat. She was thin and yellow and blinking. Her hair was wild like her mother's now, and her elbows stuck out of her clothes. She gasped when she saw René on the bench, and then me with my bloody mouth. When she spoke, it was in a whispery croak. "What are they doing awake?"

"It's earlier than usual," said Maman. "We must talk."

Behind Miriam came Madame Cauverian. While Miriam had gone sticklike, Madame Cauverian had gone flabby and pasty. She was not plump, but the tone of her flesh was poor, and there were many more wrinkles about the eyes and the corners of her mouth. She trailed a lace shawl after her and fiddled with it unceasingly. "Good evening, Madame Delarue," she said politely. "Gentlemen." If she was surprised to see us boys, she did not show it.

"Will you join us for our evening meal?" said Maman.

"How very kind," said Madame Cauverian.

And we sat down to the table, the six of us, and ate, only I couldn't eat much at all.

Madame Cauverian and Miriam talked. They talked to Pierre, about the world, about the news of the war. And Pierre answered them with specifics, with a vast fund of knowledge I didn't know he had. Maman tried to relax, but she was up and peering through the curtains every five minutes. Little by little René and I figured out what was going on.

They'd been here all along, the Cauverians. They had never left. Remember that day when Maman had sent us to the farm of Monsieur Nicodeme? And the German army had rounded up the local population of foreign Jews? Maman and Pierre had put into action the plan they had agreed on with Uncle Anton. They had hidden the Cauverians away. A full year ago! In our very home!

And for a year the Cauverians had lived in the dark, dozing and sitting silently in a space not much larger than a modern-day station wagon. They didn't dare to move in case a visitor had stopped by. They didn't dare to speak in case some neighbor needing medicine from Maman was standing down below and noticed a hushed voice overhead, a creaking floorboard. All day, in the dust and the dark, mother and daughter sat and grew thin, thinking their own thoughts.

At night, when René and I had drifted off to sleep, Maman would have Pierre remove the vases and jugs. Every night that laborious job! And every night the Cauverians would come down the ladder, and eat some food, and use the toilet at the back of the garden, and stretch their limbs, and talk to Pierre. Maman sat with them some nights. Sometimes she sat closer to our rooms, so that she would hear René and me if we stirred in our sleep. We were sound sleepers usually. That much had been a blessing.

"But why didn't you tell us?" said René, for both of us.

Maman said, "It was safer if you didn't know. Safer for everyone."

"Then why tell us now?" said René. "What's different now?"

"You must see," said Maman firmly. "You are not a stupid boy, René! You must see why you cannot have a German soldier for a friend!"

She turned to me. "And you too, Marcel!"

I was trying hard to make myself understood despite my wounds. "But Maman, why did you spit at the German soldiers in Madame Sevremont's store last year? Why did you accuse them of taking the Cauverians away? When all the time you knew they were right here?"

Maman said, "You know that Madame Sevremont. You know how she talks. I had to make sure she understood very firmly that the Cauverians were gone. If she thought so, I knew everyone else in the village would hear about it. She is better than a newspaper for spreading news. So I had to act out a scene of anger. She then had some rich, ripe gossip to pass on. I hadn't wanted anyone to know about the Cauverians in the first place, but there you are. It had gotten around—Uncle Anton learned that. So I accused the Germans of taking them."

Maman paused. "But," she continued, "I was careful I didn't call them by name. When I cursed the German soldiers that day in the pharmacy, I talked only about mothers and daughters. I knew, because I had heard, that other mothers and daughters staying near Mont-Saint-Martin had been taken. The Polish woman and her Sarah, what were their names, and the other German Jew and her baby—her *baby*, the little thing. I hoped the soldiers would see me as a woman outraged on behalf of all mothers and daughters. Only Madame Sevremont was to think I was being specific."

"Did it work?" said René, breathing lightly.

"Yes," said Pierre.

We looked at him with resentment. He had

been included in such a thrilling adventure, and he hadn't told us!

"That is, people have mentioned to me how horrible it was that my guests were taken," said Maman. "So Madame Sevremont did her part of the job very well. No one in Mont-Saint-Martin has the slightest idea that the Cauverians are still here. No one except those of us in this room."

Maman looked around at all of us.

"It is a secret that needs to be kept," she said, "until a plan for moving the Cauverians can be made. It is too early to trust anyone, though. We must wait until we are sure. And until then the Cauverians will remain our hidden guests. Is that clear?"

So *much* was clear now. Why we hadn't experienced a surplus of food once the Cauverians had disappeared. Because they were *still* eating our food, a whole year later, every night.

It was clear why I had dreamed one night that Miriam Cauverian had read Victor Hugo. *Because she had.*

It was clear why Mirabeau was gone. Because

she hadn't liked Madame Cauverian, and had always barked at her. One day she might have barked out of turn. It was too dangerous. So Maman had taken Mirabeau to the country and left her—with Monsieur Nicodeme! At this René and I blushed to remember our broad lies about how Mirabeau had died a noble death by drowning. Monsieur Nicodeme had been alerted to expect us. He had kept Mirabeau tied up and hidden in his sheep shed all day, with a rag snug around her snout to keep her from barking at our voices! As far as Maman knew, our dog was still alive and barking.

It was clear why Pierre had suddenly gone honest and stiff. Because he was nervous, entrusted with such a terrible secret. And no one to whisper it to! Poor, myopic, brave, slow-thinking Pierre, being Maman's only support! This was why he wouldn't let us steal food, of course. It meant there would be less to share with the Cauverians.

And clearest of all was why René and I could not have Monsieur Soldier as our friend.

Because even the friendliest of Germans were under orders to sniff out traitors. And we, the family Delarue, we were "traitors." Maman and her three lying little boys.

• • •

You would like, no doubt, a dramatic finale to this story. The escape of the Cauverians at last. The thrilling chase scene. The mounting violins. Everything done in tones of midnight blue and black. But of course I am not making up a story here. Real life sometimes looks like the movies. But most of the time it doesn't. It's one of your jobs as a child to learn to realize that movies often jazz things up, while real life goes by in small bits and pieces, without spotlights, without soundtracks. It is no less real for that.

22

Good-bye Gift

I saw Monsieur Soldier one more time.

It was a few weeks later. My lip had healed, and I had lost two lower teeth, which gave me a horrible, succulent lisp. When Madame Cauverian and I exchanged formal greetings every night, we sounded like steam engines passing each other. I was embarrassed by the sound of it, and I took to keeping my mouth closed.

I had gone to Madame Sevremont's shop again. I was picking up something for Maman. The old lady was adding a column of figures to tell me how much I owed. She couldn't add well, and she went over it again and again, running a finger on the left side of the column and a pencil tip on the right as if to keep the numbers from squirming around. "It's two francs and some odd centimes, but how many?" she asked herself, and started again.

The door opened, and in came my soldier.

He was dressed in a travelling coat, and he had a sack in his hands. "Well, look who I see before me," he said cheerfully. "Just the boy I was looking for."

"What's that?" said Madame Sevremont, looking up and losing her place again. She swore in a ladylike way and said, "Oh, you."

"I had a letter from my brother Karl," said my soldier. "I had told him how I would like to send him a French pastry or some sweets, but I could not. I told him all about you and your accident fishing. He wrote that I should buy some sweets for you instead. So here they are."

He juggled a small bag of hard candies, maybe four or five pieces.

"I don't accept presents from soldiers," said Madame Sevremont sternly, then added with confusing sweetness, "though it's very kind of you to offer."

"No," said the soldier. "It's for Marcel."

I looked at him. He seemed jollier than ever. "I trust you still have *some* teeth left in your mouth to eat sweets with," he said. "I didn't think I'd see you. I was going to leave these for you here and ask Madame Sevremont to give them to you the next time you were in. I'm moving out this weekend."

Oh, said my eyes.

"I can't tell you where I'm going," he said. "But I hope to see Karl and my parents before very long. I really miss my mother and my father."

Yes, I thought.

"How's crazy René?" he asked. "And the older one?"

I shrugged as if I didn't know.

He held the bag out to me. He looked hurt. It suddenly occurred to me that although he had broad shoulders and he shaved, and he carried a gun and he was a soldier in the German army, he was somehow not very different from me. I mean, he was less a grown-up than Uncle Anton, Maman, and Madame Cauverian. He was some age in between being a boy and being an adult. I had never realized such an age existed before. Perhaps

118

it's a lonely age, I thought. Especially if you're in a strange land where you can't speak the language well and everyone shuts up when you walk by.

"I wanted to say good-bye," he said. "But your mother said not to come visiting. Here you are by luck, and now I can say good-bye."

I took the bag of candy.

I thought of Madame Cauverian and Miriam in the crawl space, for fifteen months now. I thought of the danger to us all, to dear brave Maman, to stolid Pierre, to monkey-faced René, and to me. The soldier was going away now, but he might come back through Mont-Saint-Martin again. He might stop by to say hello if I was at all friendly. There was always the risk that the Cauverians could lose their lives, that Maman could be thrown into prison, that we could be separated or worse. It was too much doom for a child to imagine, yet I had to imagine it. For if I didn't, what then?

The light in my soldier's eyes seemed to dim. "I'll miss you a lot," he said, and tweaked my cheek.

I looked straight at him.

I thought of saying: *I'll miss you too.* Because I would. I thought of saying: *Good riddance, you stupid German brute.* And *that* would have been the best lie of my life so far.

But I kept my mouth shut.

For I could not speak the truth, and I could not lie.

I just held the bag of candy, twisting it between my perspiring fingers. He backed away from me awkwardly, knocking over the café chair that Madame Sevremont sometimes took to the doorway and sat in when the sun was out. His smile weakened and broke, then remade itself in a thinner, pained way. He turned and opened the door.

"Well, *au revoir*, then," he said, and left.

I never saw him again.

23
The War Ends

The Cauverians were with us for almost six more months. I grew to know them well, and realized that Miriam actually was a quick and pleasant girl. I would like to say that Madame Cauverian became agreeable and normal, but that didn't happen. Right until the day she left, she was hearing messages from angels in the sound of water running down the drains, seeing portents and omens in how the clouds were racked up across the night sky.

Eventually, when the Resistance grew stronger and more organized, she and Miriam made the daring decision to try again to make their way south into Spain. They got holed up in some other small town, however, and spent the rest of the war in hiding somewhere else. Unlike so many of their friends from Paris, they both survived the war.

Our father came home. It was not the joyful reunion we had hoped for. When in 1948 our family emigrated to the United States, it was without our father.

Aging Mirabeau came back to us and lived a happy retirement. By the time she finally died, we couldn't cry. We had cried years ago when we had held her mock funeral. Once was enough. And we were older, too. A dog's death after a good dog's life is not the most tragic thing you will witness in this world.

Once, as the war was ending, and bridges along the Loire were being blown up by retreating Germans, and the Americans and British were advancing, a column of ragged German soldiers passed through Mont-Saint-Martin. I was older now. I had gone stiff like Pierre. I had dreamed of fighting for France in the Resistance, but at twelve I was realizing that the war would be over before I could be much help. I was sitting in the café with

Pierre and René, drinking weak tea, when the soldiers came through. Though most of the patrons of the café found other things to do elsewhere, we Delarue boys stayed at our table on the pavement. Nonchalantly. We were really too frightened to say anything clever. But I looked long and hard at the faces of the soldiers, searching for the open, agreeable expression of Monsieur Soldier. The mica-glinting gray eyes, the blond hair. All I saw, alas, was the mud of war. By then no German soldier tilted his face up to scan the streets of Mont-Saint-Martin. If by some miracle of coincidence our soldier was there, as I strangely felt he might be, I did not see him.

24

The Good Liar

So then I come to the close of this rambling letter. And I must ask: Who *was* the good liar?

I began writing this intending to surprise you, as I was surprised, by my virtuous mother's surprising qualities as a liar. All the while keeping us honest, punishing us for every small fib. René and I teased her about this—many years later. At the time she would allow no teasing, and we were not so disrespectful that we would disobey.

I see Maman, still, in a black skirt and a patterned kerchief, leaning. The light falls in from the left, as in a Vermeer. (Sorry, I have tried to avoid comparing things to paintings. But I am an artist, and even a bad artist can't help trying to understand what things look like.)

In my mind Maman still leans to look out of a window. She leans to read a letter by the strong southern light. Her hands are wet from some unending household chore. She leans like a tree in soft soil, which should fall but hasn't. Now she *is* fallen, of course, folded into peace and the grave, in fancy unlikely pearls, with a rosary tucked in between her hands, hands finally dried by someone else's towel. I think those hands were wet from chores during my entire childhood. In my mind, however, she still bends, defying the law of gravity. As I said: like a tree.

In the end, though, maybe it is I who am the good liar. Or one of them. You friendly girls write to me about my childhood in wartime France. You say you have seen my paintings of bridges and trees. Perhaps I have lived too long lying to myself about how sweet my childhood was. Brave France has yet to forgive herself for falling to the Germans. For her shameful collusion in handing over so many foreign Jews (although to some extent she balked at handing over French Jews). I too must look long and hard at how those years were for so many people. I should paint my canvases not only with fields of poppies and hay wagons. What I was telling you earlier, about hearing the echoes of the past all through your life? I should listen to my own advice to you.

I should try to remember the ancient confused face of Madame Sevremont, who lived out her days on the stone steps of her pharmacy-grocery, by the end of the war too far gone to take in that it was indeed over. I might sketch the face of Monsieur Nicodeme with his beehives. Of the young schoolteacher who left to fight the invading Germans, and whose name was carved on the monument to the World War I dead when it was rededicated as a World War II memorial. I might try to paint the off-balance, crumpled rage of Madame Cauverian. Or even the three of us. Pierre, René, and me. I would like to paint us honestly, not a sentimental picture. Innocent, stupid, trusting, lying, needy, loving boys. Ordinary kids. Like you.

I have been painting not with my paintbrushes,

but with a keyboard and printer ribbons. Paint and ink, ink and paint. Because sometimes you have to *tell* the story.

Sooner or later you have to tell the story.

Miriam, who for many years has been Mrs. Delarue, has read what I have written. She objects to the part about her pelvis. She also said to tell you that her father died in a concentration camp in Poland. She thinks you should know. Otherwise she sends her love. I had asked her if *she* wanted to write this letter. She said no.

I have stayed up most of two nights to write to you. I hope you get a good grade.

Our very best wishes to you.

Sincerely,
M. Delarue

April 10

Dear Mr. Delarue,

Me and Maria and Reenie-Tawnetta got a B. Mr. Wimmel said *you* deserved the A, not us. He read your story to the whole class. Then we had to go find Mont-Saint-Martin in the atlas. Which we couldn't do. Mr. Wimmel said maybe it was too small or had become part of another town since your childhood. The atlas was from 1978. We wondered if you were being such a good liar that you made it up!

We don't care if we got a B instead of an A. We're glad you wrote to us.

Our next assignment is the Korean War. Your family didn't by any chance move to Korea in the 1950s and have any adventures there, did they?

Love,
Margaret Mueller

(I wrote something else on the back of the page. Please turn it over to see it.)

The thing I really liked about your story of your childhood, the best thing, you want to know it? It's that you didn't write yourself like a hero. You wrote yourself like a real kid. I mean, lying and all. It makes me think that history really happens to ordinary people. That history is even happening to me, right now, even if I don't know it. I like that feeling. Sometimes it's weird, like feeling so small, with outer space and infinity stretching on forever. But mostly I like it. A small speck in time, but *really here*. Thanx!